The
Third Eye
Angel Killing
Demon

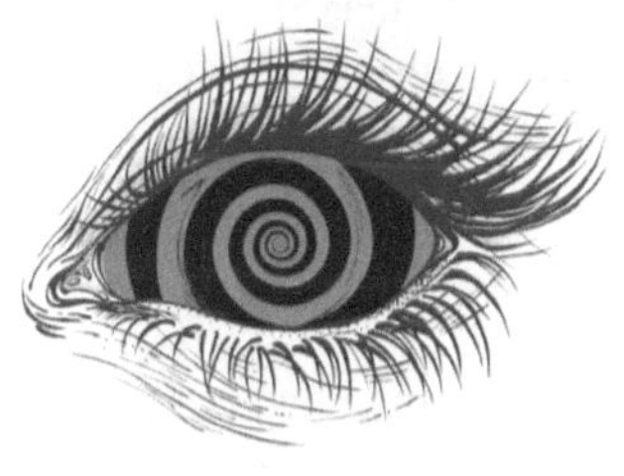

Siddhi Sethu

First published in 2020 by

Becomeshakespeare.com

Wordit Content Design & Editing Services Pvt Ltd
Unit - 26, Building A-1, Nr Wadala RTO, Wadala (East),
Mumbai 400037, India
T:+91 8080226699

©

ISBN - 978-93-89759-04-4

In fond memory of my grand parents
Smt. P.S. Ambujam and Shri A.N. Veeraraghavan

"That curse
Feared by the world
Who thought that
Would become
The light of the world."

Preface

The author has made an attempt to enlighten the people a story of a girl who has a third eye which is about insignificant and unique in understanding the story which is unbelievable but its moral can certainly be happened in anyone's life.

Fear is the key that frightens the world, but do you believe that such thing can happen in human's life.

The author is predicting that such fear psychosis can happen in anybody's life.

However, it is a fiction, but it is a world full of superstitions belief and happenings around.

The book is overall the evolution of the human mind.

Anything can happen to anybody.

But this book is about an imagination that can put anybody into thinking.

My book "The Third Eye Angel Killing Demon" is an imagination that can force anybody to think in any manner.

This book is written to weed out the fear of the mind which is the biggest enemy of the mind.

The mind works very well, and it can do a lot s of good things to the human but if it is devil, it can cause disasters. This book is an eye opener to young youth to think positively and make their life very happy.

This book has made an attempt to study the psychology of an individual and restrict to their behavior and genes of an individual.

It is therefore necessary to understand their own potentiality and lead their life happily and also peaceful.

Love and affection are the essential quality to ghostly fear and lead a perfect life which will be good to herself and the entire society.

Birth is a natural process but however if an abnormality develops, it is essential to treat abnormality right from the birth.

My book "The Third Eye Angel killing demon" is a figment of fear that creates a fear to the entire family.

Ultimately the conclusion is that even having the fear of third eye and many other things, this world accepted it and were acknowledged by each and every one.
The lots of deformities found in the human birth.
For Example:
The third eye
The stabbed poles
The monstrous strength

These are some deformities which cannot be neglected. Anything can happen in this world, but it is a research and invention and these kinds of things cannot be removed or neglected.
In conclusion, those people were acknowledged and accepted by the entire world.

From time to time, do research or invention about the psychology of a human mind.

Siddhi Sethu

Author

Acknowledgements

Name of family members `Shri P.V. Sethu, Sharada Sethu, Vinayak Sethu and Siddhi Sethu'.

My heart full thanks to my family and my people especially to my family who were there with me all this time and supported me like a hell when I was in pain.

About The Author

The author named **Siddhi Sethu** is a sweet college going girl studying in Vivekananda college of Arts, Science and Commerce. She has made serious and sincere efforts in completing the book 'The Third Eye Angel killing Demon under the circumstances beyond explanation. She has been suffering from Schizophrenia psychosis since 2014 and with this mental disease, she was able to secure 74% marks in HSC. Now she has recovered almost from this disease after miraculous struggle with this disease. Author is from a middle-class family and she is a very simple and descent person. Back then she was very untalented person and she was good at nothing but because of her sincere hard work Throughout her life, she became talented and in tenth standard, she secured 85% marks aggregate. When she was in school, she was very silent and shy girl. But because of her hard work, she has reached upto a level a that even in this condition, she was able to make a book and also, she became a skilled person. She has gone to many classes like singing class, calligraphy class, dance class, athletic class, etc. She has also completed Bharat Natyam course. She likes to sing, dance and writing books, etc. Her ambition is to become a successful writer and toeing the direction of her father who is also an author of 4 books. She wants to achieve the dream of her father who wants to become a successful and well-known writer. She considers herself as a world citizen. She wants to show everyone that she is something and want to get acknowledged by everyone. She wants to make her parents proud and for this, she always practice songs, dance and writing. She not only practice but enjoys doing it. She wants to show the entire world that she is something and wants to make her parents proud. She prays almighty God to bless her with healthy mind and body to do constructive work in life and proves herself to be an asset in life.

Foreword

The Book " The Third Eye_Angel killing Demon" is a wild imagination of the author in the 'Make believe- world.

It is, however a great honour to this young and sweet author, who could complete this book, despite she is suffering from mental dreaded disease ' Schizophrenia psychosis-since 2014.

Now that she has been recovering and under control with the support of medicine , she fought against this disease to come out of it and lead a normal life.

The book is about a girl who had a third eye and it is the life history about her and about her members who defeated an enemy and saved the entire world.

In this book, there was an old lady who ruined many people and there were some people who were ruined because of that criminal took revenge and saved the entire world.

This book deals with many scientific inventions and it is very much related to hypnotism.

We can say that it's all about people who are having super natural powers and it's how they suffered so much and finally they were acknowledged by people.

In the last ending, their supernatural powers, their deformities were accepted and they were acknowledged by the entire world.

The author has stressed upon their skills, deformities and all the scientific inventions and how they were acknowledged by the entire world and saved the world from an enemy.

Dr. Sudhir R. Chakkarwar,
B.A.M.S, D.H.A (TISS)
Piyush clinic,
Mankhurd, Mumbai-400088

Contents

The Birth of an Angel

Congratulations. You are pregnant Nina.

Nina was a young woman who was a journalist and she had a brown hair and black shiny eyes.

Nina became very happy but for some reason she was not feeling that good.

She asked to Dr. Rahul immediately about this.

Dr. Rahul was just about to say something that her husband came and showed an eye and made a very weird face towards Dr. Rahul. He was minding his own business, but Nina gotten suspicious of him and just told to her husband Max to leave.

Nina was a journalist and his husband was a scientist.

But Nina, as being a journalist was researching about people who are disabled and somethings which are related to hypnotism also.

One day she was just roaming around here and there where she figured out the falling of leaves and was just concentrated upon only and only one single leaf and she felt as if she is getting hypnotized to do that particular thing which she was focusing upon the most but for some reason, she was minding her own business.

She was happy also that she is pregnant and took care of herself very nicely. Then there came a time when she was thinking about that research about disabilities and she found lots and lots of information through that research.

She found about hypnotism a lot.
Generally for hypnotism, you need a bob of pendulum and you have to completely focus on it and then you get hypnotized.
But usually the basic logic is that you only and only have to see any vibrating object and focusing on it to get hypnotized, so instead of seeing any vibrating pendulum, see any vibrating object and think and focus only on one single thing that you want to do and immediately you will get hypnotized.
For Example: Any vibrating object such as falling of leaves, vehicle moving hereand there but the best thing to know is that you are already getting hypnotized 24 hour and you know how.
The reason is that you are seeing the vibrating object 24 hour like you move, seeing here and there, and the images of your eye sight are changing, etc Since subconsciously you are seeing moving object 24 hour and getting hypnotized, you are immediately doing those kind of things which you are thinking and focusing upon a lot.

This can be also true that even sensation also make things reality through thinking.

For Example: If you think about a sensation a lot as if you are eating something, immediately you are facing an outcome as if your stomach is filled.

Nina got to know a lot about sensation and hypnotism and somehow it can be related to disabilities also.

AFTER 6 MONTHS

Nina was walking and suddenly something weird happened to her.
She was feeling as if something was kicking her and became unconscious. She was sent to hospital and the operation started but she was little bit conscious. Her entire family came and were very worried. After the operation, the doctor comes and just say she has given birth to a baby but the way he spoken was as if he was surprised also but having very weird look.
They happily came and saw that baby and when they saw that baby, they were completely shocked.
The baby had a third eye on her forehead and she was looking very scary.

"The thought of that happiness
When that angel appeared
Became and turned into
Shocks and excitement
But came for someone
Who became a light for that M.A"

The entire family left her but Nina was the only one who took care of her and she kept her child's name Connie.

AFTER 1 YEAR

Nina was very happy cooking her meal but suddenly someone knocked the door.

When she opened the door, she gotten shocked and said one single word "W.H.Y".

The baby was kidnapped and was sent to an old lady to take care of her. She was taken care by that old lady and subconsciously she was developing her skills in practical and observational way and also developed and nurtured herself about how to use that third eye in her absence.

That old lady used to teach Connie about hypnotism and used to make her train and she gotten developed to use her hypnotism which was taught by that old lady.

An Unknown Challenge

For 9 years, everything was well and fine but she was always alone.

Then one day at the timing 8 am she was at her school. She always kept her third eye hidden with a bandage.

Teacher told her to stand and asked one single thing that why are you not studying and concentrating.

Connie only gotten interested from that one single word only and that is; WHY.

After some time, teacher told to imagine things. Connie started imagining.

Teacher said that there is a flower garden and the wind is blowing.

She felt as if she was getting hypnotized and she gotten sensation as if she is really in a flower garden and she was able to feel the wind and suddenly she fell completely unconscious that where she is and just that flower garden and wind was coming on her mind.

She was feeling as if her emotions were making her getting hypnotized and that came out to be the truth also.

Let's see how it is.

When we get emotions, we start reacting internally also and externally also. This is a kind of movement and hypnotism can occur according to how much deep our emotions are for that particular thing.

Internally our neurons react, our brain or our mind gets stressed and our glands or our hormones start reacting internally which causes the external features also.

That's how the movement occur and we can get hypnotized.

Internal stress and reactions can cause external features also.

And that's what happened to Connie also.

Connie imagined and suddenly fell down.

After she woke up, she was lying at the bed and that lady was taking care of her.

Subconsciously, she was not understanding a thing that what happened to her. But she was remembering about her past that has happened to her during past 9 years.

"Full of sadness and fear
Wanting to have an ending
But had a faith that
A light will come."

One day she was just lying on her bed and when she was just about to sleep, she suddenly thought many weird things. She imagined as if she saw someone and thought as if she and that person are going to fight.

For a moment, she was just minding her own business but suddenly she got the voice of a female and that voice made her remember something and she felt as if she knows that female.

She was not able to see it but she was able to sense it as if she needs help. For sometime she was ignoring that voice and started internally speaking to her saying "Hi". For a moment, there was no reply but after sometime, suddenly a voice came saying "Hello". Connie felt very weird for a moment but after sometime the voice disappeared.

Connie felt weird for a while but after that she thought that maybe it was her imagination.

When she was just about to sleep, something came on her mind that she is going to work in a company where she will feel very weird and confusing. But she minded her own business and slept.

In this situation, the consequences of future can also change.

The consequences of future can change but the future is set.

Time travelling can also be related to hypnotism also.

As said, how deep the focus and moving object is, that much powerful the hypnotism becomes.

When we think a lot about our future, subconsciously or consciously, we are able to do time travelling.

The same thing happened to Connie also.

Connie was able to do time travelling by listening that what is going to happen in her future and this can be related to the power of hypnotism also.

Realization of History

Connie tried to get a job somewhere but more than that her way of speaking and manners turned out to be very different than the manners she had back then.

"Lots of experiences and challenges
Turned out someone to someone
Still believing
For a light to come."

One day, she was walking here and there for finding a job but she was not getting any job.
But suddenly……

"Finding and finding
Reached to a faith
But now let's see
Whether it is a faith or curse".

She found a building which was in a very weird place. It was near Pacific Ocean and it was completely lonely and there was no sign of any one single person roaming around here and there.

It was Connie's last expectation to get a job there so she went there even though she didn't wanted to go there.

When she went to that building, she was shocked. There was no one outside but inside the building there were thousands of people working there. Although she was surprised but still she asked to a person and asked for the details about the interview and everything. He just watched and told the details but somewhere deep inside her, she was feeling very weird.

"The eye she got
Make someone to think something else
Felt as if
Related to herself."

When she was searching for the interviewer, she little bit felt weird looking the employees.

The employees were having weird looks and almost all of them were with bandages or mask or with gloves.

For some reason, she was feeling happy as if she felt that she was not the only one .

She went to the interviewer and when she saw him, she was shocked.

The interviewer was that person only whom she met before. That guy named himself James and directly selected her without asking any questions.

"The faith
Bought a realization
As if a light has came".

The most weird thing is that all the people were masked except that guy. For a while she was surprised, and she was just about to leave but by mistakably the bandage fell down and James saw that third eye on her forehead. James didn't replied anything and just gave a smile saying "WHY".
Connie was shocked and only kept on saying "WHY" all the time as if she knows this person.
James showed him very focused and rude smile to her and just told her to leave.
Connie felt very weird and just left but for some reason she was scared.

Sometimes , you realize that consciously and subconsciously you know that person but sometimes there comes a time when you never saw that person's face or seen or looked but still you understand as if you know that person.
This is actually known as blood relatives when you understand that he/she is related to her blood.
That's what happened to Connie.
She felt as if she knows James and as if that they are both blood relatives.

Ready for it

Connie listened to that voice again and there were different voices coming and she heard one single word very nicely and that word was… COME TO THE COMPANY AND ASK "WHY."

Connie smiled and immediately went to that company again.

There were lots of soldiers and all had weapons and it was a big hall where the soldiers were standing.

There were more than 3 million soldiers and when she closed her eyes, she saw I million soldiers.

3 million soldiers externally and 1 million soldiers internally and there was guy sitting nicely.

Without any fear, she saw the soldiers and came. She nicely replied that you can call me Connie.

That guy was sitting at the chair having a knife picking through his mouth.

She just replied "WHY". Connie saw the same look as she looked in James. She replied, "Hello James".

That guy gotten very angry and all the soldiers took the gun. Connie was not at all scared and when they were about to attack her, they suddenly became paralyzed.

He gotten very angry and came and tried to attack her and he also suddenly gotten paralyzed and Connie held his hands and took that knife and bite that knife and thrown it through her teeth.

"Who knew
What could have happened
Sometimes word appear
But each and everything has
A light and darkness both".

Connie replied one single thing
"D.O.N'T T.H.I.N.K T.H.A.T I A.M V.E.R.Y S.I.M.P.L.E P.E.R.S.O.N. I A.M I.M.P.R.O.V.E.R A.N.D D.O.N'T L.O.O.K A.T M.Y W.O.R.D.S A.N.D M.Y E.M.O.T.I.O.N.S, S.E.E M.Y A.C.T.I.O.N."

James smiled in a very weird and violent manner. Let's see Connie.
"WHO IS MOST DANGEROUS AND WHO IS MOST S.I.M.P.L.E….".
Let's have a fight alone together and then let's see.
Connie accepted it.
"L.E.T T.H.E P.A.R.T.Y B.E.G.I.N. S.O B.E C.H.I.L.L F.O.R N.O.W.
U.N.D.E.R.S.T.O.O.D."

Connie and James went to a lonely room.

"What a show
What a party
Let's see who is
Angel and monster."

FIGHT BEGINS

FIRST
Using weapons

James took a knife and gun and Connie took a defence weapon and a very strong gun.

JAMES FIGHTS
"Knife thrown in different angles
Gun continuously
Muscles to FEAR
No need for DEFENCE
skilled to fear ".

CONNIE FIGHTS
"Guns in different angles
weapons for defence
Taken help to
ATTACK AND DEFENCE
Long hair to ATTACK
Skilled to confuse".

Connie comes and keep her legs straight in right angle in front of James. Now Connie comes and sees him very weirdly and violently. James gotten shocked and seeing her as if it is related to his life in some or the other way.

"PARTY GOES TO CONNIE".

James asked "WHO ARE YOU? WHAT ARE YOU ?
She didn't replied a thing and just left smilingly and she just said that she is ready to help you.
A.R.E Y.O.U R.E.A.D.Y F.O.R I.T?
James gotten shocked and cried happily.

AFTER 8 YEARS

8 years has passed. James became strong externally and became good at physical activities. His name became SMOSH. Connie became strong in observation, stubbornness and mastered how to use that third eye and also she was good at smart fighting by hitting only on a person's weak points and especially her skills in hypnotism. Her name became VOSS.
SMOSH became good at physical strength and became most powerful and rude and VOSS became good at observation, pointing on a person's weak points and mastered how to use third eye and became very beautiful having a very long hair.
Both of them said one single word.

"W.E A.R.E R.E.A.D.Y F.O.R I.T S.O W.A.I.T F.O.R 6 Y.E.A.R.S T.O E.N.J.O.Y T.H.E P.A.R.T.Y".

SMOSH had 50,000 external soldiers and 3 million internal soldiers and VOSS had 100,000 external soldiers and 1 million internal soldiers plus her own strength that is; her observation and stubbornness.
They had to find those 6 people who are going to help them to defeat that criminal.
THEY MADE A PLAN ABOUT A WORLD TOUR AND GOTTEN SEPARATED TO FIND THAT CRIMINAL and THOSE 6 PEOPLE.

The story of a monster

"CHALLENGE FOR JAMES"

James went to some top touristic places famous all over the world which are;
The Maasai Mara National Reserve, Kenya?. Japan Sydney

THE MAASAI MARA NATIONAL RESERVE, KENYA

SMOSH went to airport and reached Kenya. He was in a car and when he was about to reach the Maasai Mara National Reserve, he saw a lady who was continuously looking at her very weirdly.
James was doing world tour to find those criminals who were changing his/her faces and same was for Connie.
He reached to the Maasai Mara National Reserve. When he was coming there he met a person. That person looked to be a very strong man. For a while, he was suspicious of him but he casually talked to him and he realized that he was very traditional and always talked about god.

He minded his own business that time but when he saw him he was looking at him and that person said his name,"M.O.S.T".

SMOSH was trying to understand that person. He was looking and observing his way of talking and figured out that whenever he was talking about god his left hand was shivering a little bit.

SMOSH smiled very rudely and thought about something.

"Bad or Good

It will come

So …….

BABY LET THE GAMES BEGIN

READY FOR IT".

He was ready to stay with that person and said one single word I.e., "M.A"

'M: Money maker'

'A: Am'

SMOSH gotten very very angry and started beating that person saying that you are using god and gave that person a very severe punishment. "M.O.S.T"

'M: Money maker

O: Observation .

S: Smartness

T: Traditional

SMOSH beaten and improved him in such a way that

'M: You are a MONSTER because you used them

O: Become an ORDINARY person or else……

S: Remember your SCARY face forever

T: Don't even TRY to use anyone or I will…….

SMOSH immediately asked to that person that have you improved or should I show a very very rude look to you.

His eyes were red and full of danger.

M.O.S.T's left hand shivered and answered that ya I am using god but what's the big deal and I hope that you are that person only who has come back again to save this world. So, get ready cause you are chosen, and your life made by that enemy is going to begin again now. So, get ready now.

SMOSH asked that how you know about this.

M.O.S.T replied that I know that enemy in some or the other way and I am going to tell you my story that what happened to me.

A long while ago when I was a child, I had a supernatural ability and that is; I had a monstrous strength easy enough to destroy the entire land.

I got this monstrous strength only and only because my genes were very strong, and my muscles and I have a very monstrous and strong ability.

Everything was going well and fine but suddenly I met a woman and that woman was looking very very sympathetic.

I was not able to show my skills and my monstrous strength only and only because I was feeling sympathetic towards her. That was the starting of my hell.

Whatever she used to say, I used to do and that made me a Monster.

I was angry with god only and only because why it happened to me only and I stopped beating people because I wanted to be a sympathetic person back then and now she made a future and I did everything accordingly as written in future.

That was the reason it killed my heart and because of her future which was set for me ruined me. But SMOSH said only one single word and that was;

"Future is set
Decision is made
Now its time to start
And ready to face."

That day has begun finally now.

SMOSH was resting like that only and thinking that the day has come to finally reveal the truth to him himself only.

Usually people say that strong people are very egoistic people but for some reason, egoistic people is needed.

If you don't find egoistic people, then how will you be able to understandyourself and them.

Sometimes having sympathy towards other people and trying to help them sometimes it harms yourself.
Having sympathy for someone is ok but not that much.
This world doesn't like sympathetic people that much.

35

Truth is revealed

ALONG YEARS AGO

How are you James?
Feeling fine now.
James replied that Ya I am fine.
I will take care of you forever. Understood.
James asked,"WHY?".
It's simple because you are me only.

James was so happy hearing this and immediately said to that person that I want you to stay inside of me forever. That person with whom James was talking was looking as if…

"Looking as if
Angel from inside
But finally, the reality was
Devil stayed inside that angel
FOREVER."

CONNIE… HOW ARE YOU? WHAT ARE YOU DOING?

THE TRUTH IS THAT I AM YOUR M.A .
I AM GOING TO TELL YOU EVERYTHING NOW
THE ONLY REASON THAT I LEFT YOU WAS
BECAUSE OF A REASON THAT HAS CAME
ALIVE NOW TO RUIN US and I am……

James

'J: JEALOUSY was
A: ACCEPTED by me
M: formed me into a MONSTER
E: or ELSE
S: would have lived a SIMPLE life'

AND THE ENEMY IS A PERSON WHO HAVE
ONLY AND ONLY THESE 5
QUALITIES AND i.e.,

COMPARISON
GREEDY
JEALOUSY
HATRED
PAIN

And the enemy calls itself as….
C.G.H.J.P
THE SHOCKING TRUTH IS:
JAMES is NINA.

MISSION : WORLD UNITY

A long back years ago humans didn't used to know anything when this world gave birth to them.
There are five people who changed them into an untalented person to a talented person.

{For surviving,
They need food (Farmers)
For their health,
They need medical facilities which are already given by (Doctors)
For their protection,
They need (Police)
For gaining knowledge,
They were trained by (Teachers)
For expressing their skills and to be acknowledged by everyone, They need supporters (World Citizens)}

When everything started? Who knows?
Hey… How are you? Are you okay? Someone has come to meet you.
Understood.
Hi Nina. Are you feeling okay now? I have come to pick you up. Let's go….

That was the time when everything started.
I always think that only….. WHY?
When you came?

How you came?
Y…….

AFTER 1 YEAR

Everything was going very normal. There was an old lady who always used to
take care of her.
Things were looking very good and well.
One day when she was sleeping, she heard a voice which was coming inside of her.
First time she gotten little bit surprised but afterwards she started talking to that voice but for some reason she ignored that voice.

THAT WAS THE STARTING OF MY CHALLENGE

What is happening to me? Why I am feeling that way? Who knows?
That old lady was cooking her meal. There were many things that she made. For some reason Nina was feeling very weird because very weird things were coming on her mind as if she was comparing different things and as if she was getting angry looking to those things which were better than her and something came which was named as comparison. She was asking the reason to herself "WHY?".

W: When you came?

H: How you came?
Y: You…

She kept on asking this question again and again.
Then one day she was having a walk like that only.
Whoever she was seeing, she started comparing them.

"A darkness came
The beginning of Darkness
Started with comparison
Beginning of the challenge."

After 10 years:

"Comparison came into reality
Reality came into
BELIEF
Accepted by everyone."

For 10 years she developed herself in such a way that she started comparing everyone with herself to see whether who is good and who is bad. But she always took things very positively.
Comparing them in such a way that it makes everyone to improve themselves and to start taking things very positively.

BELIEF came as if everything or everyone are NOT that good and NOT that bad.

Then one day to make herself more and more improved she developed her
skills and she started doing lots of work.
When she was doing work, she started becoming more and more greedy to do that work.
She was not able to stop herself to do her work.
She was walking here and there wanting to do any work.
Suddenly she fell like to do any work and she became greedy for everything and became a 24 hardworking person.

"A wish
To do anything
Not able to control
Given a birth named
Greediness".

After 10 years:

For 10 years, Nina took help from her greediness to think or wanting to do good intentional things.

"Greediness came into reality
Brought out a positivity
WANTING TO DO SOMETHING
Good for everyone".

Then one day when she was doing her day to day life activities ,she saw some people who were doing their work better than her and she was getting jealous seeing them but for some reason she was minding her own business. She was thinking of doing her work better than their work and she started doing her work even more nicely and confidently.

"Judging and judging
Came a time
To do anything
Gave rise to
Jealousy".

For 10 years, she accepted this jealousy to keep on doing things more and more better than anyone else could have done and kept on doing good intentional things.

"Jealousy came into reality
Brought out a chance
TO KEEP ON DOING THINGS
To develop and improve skills".
Then one day there came a time when she met a person named Max and for some reason when she was seeing him, she started hating that man and she felt as if she was being hated by him.
For some days, everything was going well. Then one day there came a time when those two met each other and for some reason Nina gotten little bit attracted towards him and vice versa.

At first, they were silent and they were not talking to each other at all.

One day Max tried to come to talk to her, but that old lady came and picked Nina and she left.

That time Max was following her and for some reason she was getting irritated but still she was minding her own business.

She was hating him but deep inside her heart she was feeling good also.

"Whatever we feel
Hate or love
There comes a truth
Having emotions for them".

Time passed and they fell in love with each other.
WE PEOPLE SAY THAT LOVE IS BLIND. WHY…?

"LOVE is blind
it is a kind of angel
Who doesn't need any senses?
It directly comes through feelings".

Then one day there came a time when they were alone, and they fell like kissing each other and Nina became pregnant. To not get any insult Nina and Max secretly married with each other.

The only ones who knew about it was that old lady and Max's father.

For many months everything was going well, and they were happy.
Then a child was born and that child was Connie.

Then there came a time when she was happily cooking her meal although she was alone and her entire family left her and for her only her daughter Connie was important to her and when she was doing her work someone knocked the door.

She gotten shocked and that person who came was Max.
Max was nervous and Nina gotten shocked that why you came.
Max came and told her the entire truth to her.

IT WAS ME NINA. IT WAS ME.
I KNOW THE TRUTH ABOUT YOUR DAUGHTER CONNIE.

Your daughter Connie was experimented by me. When you were pregnant, I
experimented your body.
Because of me only your daughter has gotten a third eye on her forehead and she looks scary.
It was me only who told Dr. Rahul to experiment and I gave him money also.
There was a reason behind it why I did that.
The reason is your aunt that is; your old lady.

Max told the entire truth to her. When I was stalking you when you were there with your aunt, your aunt gave me a very weird look and then I don't know why, I suddenly fell in love with you.

It was as if I was hypnotized to love you.

Then when we married secretly, my father told the truth to your old aunt and my dad was tortured by your aunt.

Still I was not able to believe that, and I kept on loving you like a hell.

Then there came a time when I was alone, and I was hypnotized seeing your aunt. I myself don't know how and why? Then I went to Dr. Rahul and told him to experiment your body.

THE EXPERIMENT WAS…

There was an eye which was preserved. That eye was a living eye and if it is living, it must be containing some genes. When that egg was forming, that eye was being swallowed by your mouth and those genes made the changes in egg and the baby came with a third eye on her forehead.

All the genetic features changed completely, and the baby was born named Connie.

"A family bond
A family relationship
Broken into pieces
Because of one single
Mistake".

WHY THIS HAS HAPPENED?
HOW THIS HAS HAPPENED?
WHEN THIS HAS HAPPENED?
WHO KNOWS.

James was thinking like that only and before he was about to begin again his challenge, he said one single word and that was;
I HAVE CAME AND I WILL DEFINITELY TAKE REVENGE FOR MY DAUGHTER
AND WITH YOU.
UNDERSTOOD.

The Regret of Becoming a Beauty

JAPAN

SMOSH reached Japan and he was seeing the place. The place was very good, and he reached a place where there was a garden which was full of cherry blossoms. He went there and he saw a girl who was standing in middle of garden and cherry blossoms trees all over spreading here and there. It was looking very calm, chill and the most beautiful scenery.

He met that girl and when he saw that girl, he was little bit shocked.

She was looking the most beautiful girl he had never seen in his entire life. He asked about the details or information from that girl. That girl named herself as G.A.B.E.

SMOSH asked to introduce yourself.

That girl replied,

"Kon ni chi wa{Hello}.

Watashino name wa G.A.B.E. desu"{"My name is G.A.B.E".}.

SMOSH asked ,"Eigo ga hanasemasuka?"{"Can you speak English?"}.

G.A.B.E. replied," Eigo ga hanasemasu"{ " I can speak English"}.

She replied in English.

What is your name and what are you doing here?

He replied, "My name is SMOSH and I want some information about something and that's why I am doing a world tour. Only this much."

I am G.A.B.E. I would like to talk to you a little bit about something and I want to help you in that.
For some reason, GABE started flirting him and SMOSH was minding his own business.
SMOSH nicely said that I am a woman.
GABE gotten shocked saying that you are a woman and you clearly look like a man and what happened to you and how you became like that.
SMOSH nicely answered that I have a reason how I became like that and it's something which is very painful for me.

For some reason, GABE understood SMOSH and said that I am ready to help you.
I am going to tell you about my life history and maybe

hearing this, you can get some help related to your mission of doing a world tour.

A long back years ago, I met a man. If you want to know about me myself a little bit, I am known to be the most beautiful person having a very very long hair and I can be said as "Queen of Beauty".
But because of some reason, I hate beauty.
SMOSH gotten little bit surprised saying that why you hate beauty even knowing that almost everyone likes to become the most beautiful person and you already are so why are you upset then.
GABE said only and only one single word and that is; no doubt that people always chase after beauty but forget the value of getting true friends. Now I am going to tell you what happened to me back then.
I met a man and subconsciously I fell in love with him. He always used to help me in each and every thing and one after the other time, my love for him went even more deeply.
Everything was going on very well but after that something happened to me afterwards which turned my entire life into hell.
That man expected a lot from me, and I kept on doing things that he wanted to do from me.
I did each and everything that he wanted, and you know what happened to me…
BETRAYAL
USE

This is what I got………..
I did so much for him, and this is what I gotten.
How pitiful…..
This is what happened to me and I know some details about something. I will give you one clue and that is;

When we try to do lots and lots of things, our expressions and our identity changes.
There are 2 different forms of people but actually there is only and only one single thing.

Hearing this, SMOSH suddenly became shocked and gotten panic.
He asked that who are you.

She replied that I am G.A.B.E.:
G: I am considered as GODLY figured person.
A: I am being ACCEPTED to stay in this world.
B: I am the most BEAUTIFUL person.
E: This is the truth which is accepted by the ENTIRE world.

I HAVE CAME HERE TO HELP YOU TWO. UNDERSTOOD.

SMOSH gotten shocked but for some reason he was happy internally also. He became very happy and told to her that I will definitely come to see and meet you again.

The Angry for Beggars

SYDNEY

SMOSH reached Sydney and was trying to gather some information about the place. It was the most populous city no one ever knew about it.

He was nicely trying to see the city and was feeling very very excited to know about this place.

Then there was a crowd and SMOSH was surprised that why there are so many crowds here and there.

There came a guy who was walking very bravely and it seemed as if he was the most richest man and that turned out to be the truth also.

That man saw SMOSH and pointed immediately towards him and said one single word to him and came very close saying that…

IF THERE IS A PURPOSE, THERE WILL COME A PARTNER ALSO TO SUPPORT THAT PERSON TO FULFILL HIS/HER GOAL.

SMOSH immediately understood that the criminal has a partner also.

He gave one sign and gently asked his name and his description to that rich person.

That man replied that his name is GROSS, and he told about him himself in this way:

G: I am a GODLY figured person.
R: I am the most RICHEST man.
O: I have good OBSERVANCE.
S: I am the STRONGEST person.
S: I am the most SMARTEST person.

SMOSH gently asked that who are you and what you want from him. GROSS nicely said, "Listen to me very closely now. I am going to say to you something which is going to make you to get shock."

GROSS nicely said that there are 6 people who are going to help you to fight with that criminal out of which one is me.

SMOSH nicely said that I have met 2 of them already and he asked that how you know about this.
GROSS nicely said I am one of them and I was the strongest and this is the reason I know everything about it.

Before going I am going to tell you about me myself

and I will get in contact with each and everyone and going to bring them to you. And now I am going to tell you about my life history.

I was from a very rich family from the very beginning and we had a very happy life together.
Then there came a time when I was just walking here and there and found a person who was looking very poor and begging for food.
I thought of helping her and that was the biggest mistake that I did that time.
Even now also I hate beggars.
I feel like killing them when they beg for mercy.

So, I thought of helping her and I helped her also.

All the time she was begging for money and told me how to use it.
I was helping her by giving her money all the time and made securities to safeguard her.
That was the biggest mistake I did in my entire life.
Very very smart person she is.

Used me very nicely and took securities also and money also. Somehow, I became a company owner and became the most richest man.
But even now also I feel like killing all those beggars.
I always think that instead of begging for money, why can't they use this much energy to work for their needs.

This is my entire life history and details about me and that poor woman.

SMOSH understood the details about that criminal from each and every person from everyone and found out each and every person are going to help them fighting that enemy and came back to wait for Connie to come.

CHALLENGE FOR JAMES IS OVER.

Life History About Connie

"CHALLENGE FOR CONNIE"

WHEN THIS ALL STARTED.
WHY ONLY ME.
HOW EVERYTHING CHANGED THAT MUCH.
WHO KNOWS….
THE ENTIRE STORY STARTED FROM HERE….

The baby was kidnapped and was sent to an old lady and that baby was Connie. For some years, she was completely taken care by her old aunt for 9 years.

HOW I FACED THAT? WHO KNOWS?

"The hell that came
Who knows why it came
But definitely one thing sure
Everything comes for a valid
REASON".

Throughout those past 9 years, lots of things happened.

LOTS OF CHALLENGES.
LOTS OF EXPERIENCES.
LOTS OF MOMENTS.
WHEN THIS THING BEGAN, WHO KNOWS?

Connie had a third eye which was lying in her forehead and because of this her hell began.
She was always criticized and ostracized by others and she was being called a monster by everyone.

"The demon that lies
Was not agreed by that angel
Who accepted that demon
As a light for her".

She started remembering each and everything that happened to her throughout these past 9 years.
The only one who was taking care of her was that old lady and she became light for her.
She was giving her food, shelter, cloth and to hide that third eye, she hidden that third eye by using bandages.
She gave her everything that no one can give it to anyone and because of that old aunt she was allowed to go to school and doing her day to day life activities even though her third eye was hidden.

For Connie, her old aunt became light for her.
Everything was going well and fine.

Then one day, her teacher told her to imagine things and she followed it verynicely.

WHO KNOWS WHAT HAPPENED TO ME THAT TIME?
NOW I AM UNDERSTANDING EVERYTHING NOW.
I DIDN'T SLEPT THAT TIME, I SUBCONSCIOUSLY DIED THAT TIME AND CAME BACK ALIVE FROM MY SUBCONSCIOUS DEATH.

Then Connie was just lying on her bed and she heard a voice and imagined many things.

NOW I UNDERSTOOD THE TRUTH.
THAT FEMALE'S VOICE WAS THE COMBINATION OF HER OLD AUNT AND NINA.
AM I UNDERSTANDING THE FUTURE WHICH IS GOING TO COME TO ME?

AFTER 10 YEARS

Connie's manners and her way of speaking completely changed. Back then she was very simple and innocent person but now she became very brave and smart but still her way of speaking was kind.

"Manners changes
Accordingly, the way

The environment is but
Each and every behavior
Has a value and its importance".

She was searching for a job and she found a place which was near to the Pacific Ocean and she went there even though she didn't wanted to. She saw many people who were looking very weird and their way of speaking was completely different. Then she met James and they had a very complicated meeting where her secret that she has a third eye on her forehead was revealed and she was directly selected by James who showed very rude smile to her.

THE SECRET WAS THIS.
WHATEVER SHE IMAGINED AND SHE HEARD, IT WAS COMING TRUE AS IF SHE WAS SEEING THE FUTURE.
JAMES AND CONNIE WERE SOMEHOW INTERLINKED.
NO SURPRISE EVEN THOUGH SHE HAD A THIRD EYE AS IF HE KNOWS THAT GIRL.

AFTER 5 YEARS

HEARD A VOICE…
"Come to the company and ask WHY…".
3 MILLION EXTERNAL SOLDIERS AS HIS BODYGUARDS AND 1 MILLION INTERNAL SOLDIERS TO FIGHT.

There was a gate where no one was allowed to go and there were lots of security guards also.

There were many secret and hidden weapons and passwords to punish if someone enters.

Connie had a very beautiful face and she had a curly long hair and her nails are sharp, her forehead was covered with bandages and her eyes were cruel. She was able to enter the gate and the way she entered was awesome:

Security guards: Connie showed her beauty.

Secret and hidden weapons: She was able to go through that by using her third eye and her observational and fighting skills.

Passwords: Connie asked some of the internal soldiers and through their murmur and the reaction they showed, she was able to remove the password also and the password was "CHLNRSST."

THE PASSWORD WERE THE SKILLS OF THOSE PEOPLE WHO ARE GOING TO FIGHT WITH THAT ENEMY.

CHLNRSST:

C: Crazy person. H: Handsome man.

L: Long haired woman.

N: Nature follows him.

R: Rich man.

S: Uses weapons which are stabbed on that person's body.
S: Strong person.
T: Having a third eye.

THESE ARE THOSE PEOPLE WHO HAVE THESE ABILITIES AND ARE READY TO FIGHT WITH THAT ENEMY.

Finally Connie came to that place where that man was nicely sitting having a knife on his mouth and showing his attitude judging everyone very rudely.

"What a rude behavior
But finally, an angel came
To remove the ego
from that man who is caught by
An egoistic demon".

FINALLY COMES
CONNIE….
SAYING VERY CASUALLY
"HELLO JAMES".

James gotten very angry and was about to stab her with a knife but as everyone knows:

"Anger does nothing
Doesn't give any solution

Accept giving harm to others
Especially themselves".

Connie nicely says to James that you are nothing accept
showing your anger and ego.
RIGHT…….

"With no fear
Biting that knife
So sharp to give it a scar
Showing that smile
Which removes that ego and anger
IMMEDIATELY".

TIME FOR FIGHT.
ARE YOU READY FOR IT…?

"What a fearful body
What an anger
What an attack
Make others to listen to
HIM".

"What a smartness
What a defence
What a confusing strategy
To attack
To make others bow in front of
HER".

PARTY BEGINS.
GAME OVER.
WINNER IS CONNIE.
LET'S GO….

Connie sees him very violently.
James sees her very shockingly.
THE TRUTH IS THAT I ALREADY KNOW THAT YOU ARE MY MOTHER. SEEING VERY VIOLENTLY BECAUSE WHY YOU BETRAYED ME? SEEING VERY SHOCKINGLY THAT HOW YOU UNDERSTOOD THAT….?

The enemy is that old lady, right. I know everything already. Don't worry.
I am going to help you by killing that enemy.
This is my decision. Understood. Let's go….

AFTER 8 YEARS

James changed his name and named himself as SMOSH.
S: Strong
M: Money maker
O: Observation
S: Smartness
T: H: Looking like a Head

Connie named herself as VOSS.
V: Violent

O: Observation
S: Strong
S: Smartness

SMOSH had 50,000 external soldiers and 3 million internal soldiers and VOSS had 10,000 external soldiers which were previously the soldiers for SMOSH and 1 million internal soldiers which were very strong, and VOSS also had stubbornness and observational skills.

NOW IT'S MY TURN TO FACE THE CHALLENGE BY FINDING THOSE PEOPLE WHO ARE GOING TO HELP THEM TO FIGHT WITH THAT CRIMINAL.

NOW THE CHALLENGE BEGINS…

The Violence of Comedian

MEXICO

Connie reached Mexico and was roaming around here and there. When she was roaming here and there, she saw a shop where she went and when she was about to buy something ,she saw a man who was calling someone and he was making jokes one after the other time. Everyone were looking at him very weirdly but he was minding his own business and one after the other jokes he kept on making.

Connie saw him and she smiled at him minding her own business.

That guy was very weird and very funny person and his face was very weird and comical.

When Connie finished drinking her coffee, she went to meet that guy. She casually asked that when you know that everyone were laughing and weirdly looking at you, why you were acting so weirdly.

He minded his own business and started making weird jokes:
A good and kind person fell in love and started helping the enemy {Good people doing bad}.
Everyone tries to change the future but future was decided from the very starting {Thought of changing didn't happened at all}.
There are many faces, but the person is one {One person having different faces}.
N. Emotionless things gotten emotions {Material have gotten emotions}.

Connie became suspicious and gently asked," What is your name?"
My name is CAGE and I accept that I am like that and I am warning you not to change me. He saw Connie very rudely as if he has a purpose of becoming like that and having that kind of behaviour. He revealed also that how he is alike.

C: COMEDIAN.
A: ACCEPTED the way he is.
G: GODLY figured.
E: very EGOISTIC person.

CAGE replied that you know each and every comedian look very funny, but they have a pain, they have a violence that is lying inside of them.
What you think, it really makes sense for you all as if

we like to make jokes, we like to be comical, but the answer is not.

We comedians also have a pain, a violence that we are hiding and it still lies inside of us and whenever we think about it, it hurts.

CAGE started crying and started saying that I want revenge from that person who made me like this, who pulled me out into a situation like this. I will make comedy jokes in front of her so much so much that she will badly crying laughingly will die.

VOSS nicely smiled and understood his pain and just said one single word and that is; I was the same person back then but for some reason I don't want to say how my behaviour is now.

VOSS replied that tell me your story about how everything happened and what exactly happened to you.

CAGE answered saying that fine I am ready to say what exactly happened to me because of that bitch.

Back then, I always wanted to become a comedian and I was not really good at making jokes.

Then there came a lady who said to me that she will train me to become an extra ordinary comedian.

I believed blindly towards her and thinking that I will become a good comedian and kept on making jokes, but those jokes were related to: USE

MURDER

KILL
CRIME

And you know what she did to me, she immediately criticized me for each and everything and revealed in front of the entire world that I am a violent comedian.

Now I want to take revenge with her and want to show that how a real violent comedian reacts with each and everyone.

VOSS revealed her name and just casually asked that are you ready to come to help me.
CAGE accepted and just said,"YES….".
VOSS gotten excited and understood that he has a contact with that criminal, and she left and minded her own business.

The Magic of Being Handsome

Connie reached New York and as soon as she reached, she saw that there were many people who were gathering and there came a man who was looking so handsome that all the people started shouting and screaming and all the girls were chasing after him although Connie was looking normal seeing him.

That man saw her and tried to flirt her, but she was minding her own business.

That man came to her and gently asked that what is your name.

She normally replied her name that is; VOSS and asked his name also.

He very casually and gently said his name that my name is HAG.

He in a flirtatious way said that you know I am very annoyed of other girls but still I will tell you about me myself:

HAG started flirting her and that made VOSS very angry and showed a very cruel eye.

HAG told her to be very casual saying that be chill, girl. I am a very casual man and you can be casual to me so don't worry. He introduced himself in this way:

H: HANDSOME man.
A: ANNOYED of girls.
G: GODLY figured person.

He said about his city that is; New York and told many details about his country: New York known as the most populous city, densely populated major city in United States. This country is world's most populous megacities, important center for international diplomacy, largest foreign born population and the home to the highest number of billionaires and I the most handsome man stay in such a country and I am extremely proud of it.

VOSS in a very suspicious way saw him and very gently showed an eye.

Then HAG kept on saying and saying.
Each and every country has its own value and importance and one of them is New York and I am proud that I stay in this world.
VOSS gotten impressed hearing his words and minded her own business and just asked one single word and that was; what exactly you want from me.
He minding his own business tried to flirt her, but

VOSS showed such a bad look to him that he gotten normal but flirtatiously smiling at her and talking about this world.

He was saying in such a way that as if he wants to stay in this world and always want to protect this world from each and every enemy who tries to ruin it.

He gently replied only one single thing that is; the magic of being handsome is going to show you someday for sure, no doubt about it.

VOSS was about to leave but before that HAG told one single word that I will do anything to protect this world.

VOSS before leaving wanted to ask lots of detail about him.

HAG gently asked," Do you want to flirt me now?"
VOSS said, "I have no interest to flirt you. I just want to know about you. I know that you are saying lie. Tell me what are your intentions".

HAG very freely and casually said that you know I love this world because I exist, otherwise no other reason.

You know what being the most handsome man is like being in a hell.

All the time only and only flirtations, they just want my body not my feelings.

Only this much I wanna say.

VOSS felt as if his way of reacting and his flirtatious nature has gotten a reason behind it and also it is the correct answer also and it is something which is related to save the world or saving himself existing in this world.

Who is Nature's True Lover?

PARIS

VOSS reached Paris and started seeing the places. She felt very good and felt nice seeing these places.

She was gathering lots of information about this country.

This country is especially known for its museums and architectural landmarks. This country has attracted artists from around the world and acquired a reputation as the "City of Art".

She was nicely sitting in a bench. The leaves were falling, and everything was very beautiful and she was wondering that even this nature is also like an art.

"NATURE
What an art
What a beauty
That makes the entire world
So peaceful and beautiful".

Suddenly she saw a man who was roaming around here and there and when he was roaming, automatically the leaves started falling and the wind came, and everything was looking so good and calm.

VOSS was looking at him and whenever the trees and plants he was observing, he was one after the other bowing and looking at him VOSS smiled at him.
She went and started talking to that guy and just asked that are you a nature lover.
He felt very happy and suddenly said his name and started talking about nature.

"My name is GAN",he said. He told about himself as:

G: GODLY figured person.
A: APPRECIATING nature.
N: a true NATURE lover.

He was talking about nature a lot saying that the nature is so beautiful and nature is everything.
Nature gives life.
Nature gives shelter.
Nature is like our home.
Nature is everything.
ESPECIALLY FOR ME.

He immediately talked to her that if nature is not there, then nothing is there and I am proud to be called as a nature lover.

VOSS smiled and casually said that if nature gives us everything, then what was that moral that was said by everyone that nature is cruel.

"The true lover
That heard the criticism about their important ones
The anger that raised higher
Made that lover to loose emotions ".

GAN gotten very angry and immediately rain occurred, thunder storm began and leaves started falling very crazily.

HOW DARE YOU INSULT MY
IMPORTANT ONES
THE ONE WHO IS EVERYTHING TO ME.
I WILL KILL YOU
RIGHT HERE, RIGHT NOW.

The anger that came made the entire environment scary and dangerous.
GAN completely became mad and started fighting with VOSS.

"The true lover for nature
Made him angry
Seeing the insult of that heaven
Which is everything for him".

"Insult is known as wrong thing

But everything has a reason
Which is
NOT THAT GOOD
NOT THAT BAD".

GAN was about to kill VOSS but VOSS showed such
a look that even nature gotten scared including GAN.

"What a look
what a face
What an eye
Made danger to dangerous person
To get scared".

VOSS left but before going, she said one single word
and that is;

"Nature is cruel
Because they have emotions
But this world doesn't bother
If they wouldn't had
EMOTIONS".

GAN gotten impressed and just said internally that I
am ready to help you anytime and any moment.

VOSS just gave him an offer that if you are so fond of
nature, you and your nature can help me in defeating
one criminal and left.

CHALLENGE FOR CONNIE IS OVER.
THOSE PEOPLE ARE FOUND.
SHE REACHED FINALLY.

Upcoming of All The Members

FINALLY COME ALL THOSE PEOPLE WHO ARE GOING TO HELP US TO DEFEAT THAT ENEMY.

CAME.......

MOST
GABE.
GROSS.
HAG
GAN.
CAGE.
VOSS.
SMOSH

WE 8 PEOPLE ARE GOING TO FIGHT WITH THAT ENEMY INCLUDING INTERNAL AND EXTERNAL SOLDIERS.
TELL THE DETAILS AND YOUR ABILITIES…
NOW…

>. MOST

I am from Kenya and I have a contact with that criminal. That criminal ruined my life and that's why I behaved as if I am very normal and traditional person but actually I was blaming me myself and I am going to help you to defeat and kill that enemy.

I am a very strong person. I am so strong that I can break the land and I am a money maker also.

?. GABE

I am from Japan and I can speak English and Japanese both. I have a contact

with that criminal because subconsciously I fell in love with that enemy. My abilities are that I am a very strong and beautiful person.

I have gotten very very long hair and I can fight with that enemy by using my long hair.

@. GROSS

I am from Sydney and I am a very very rich person. I was the one who gave money to that enemy because I gotten sympathetic towards that enemy and I Can help you in fighting with that enemy by taking help from my securities and bodyguards.

N. HAG

I am from New York and I am the most handsome man you would have never seen in your entire life.

I gotten in contact with that enemy because I used to

flirt that enemy and I am going to fight with that enemy by showing my handsome face and make that enemy's partner as my partner and defeating that enemy.

O. GAN

I am from Paris and I am a true Nature lover and I can do anything to save my Nature.

I am going to help you to defeat that enemy by taking help from my Nature and killing that enemy who wants to ruin my Nature.

P. CAGE

I am from Mexico and I like to make jokes with everyone. I had a contact with that enemy only and only because I used to share my jokes with that enemy also and I became a laughing stock.

I want to kill that enemy because that person ruined my life by making me a laughing stock in front of the entire world and I want to kill her by making so many jokes so that the enemy will be requesting me to kill itself.

Q. VOSS

I am VOSS and my actual name is Connie. I have a third eye on my forehead, and I was taken care by that enemy only and I am now going to defeat that old lady. I also have gotten some internal and external soldiers.

R. SMOSH

I am SMOSH and my real name is James. That enemy has hypnotized me and my entire body is with rods being stabbed here and there. I can fight with that enemy by using those stabbed rods which are being stabbed in my body here and there.

WE ALL ARE GOING TO FIGHT THAT ENEMY. UNDERSTOOD……REPLY FROM OTHERS

GOT IT……
LET'S GO
SMOSH AND VOSS
GABE AND HAG
MOST AND GAN
GROSS AND CAGE.

One day SMOSH AND VOSS were walking like that only and SMOSH took her to a lonely place where he revealed that I am your mom Nina who has came into this form as a boy.

VOSS didn't replied a word and was about to mind her own business but SMOSH stopped and said immediately that I need to talk to you. I know that how you gotten that third eye on your forehead.

I AM YOUR MOM NINA.
I KNOW WHAT HAPPENED TO YOU.
I KNOW THAT HOW YOU GOTTEN THIS THIRD EYE

AND WHY YOU GOTTEN THAT THIRD EYE.

A long time ago, I was also taken care by an old lady and that old lady is the criminal.
That old lady used to take care of me also. There was a time when I heard the voice. She named herself as C BIRTH.
That was the starting of my challenge.
I always used to get different kinds of feeling each and every time.
Comparison
Greediness.
Jealousy

All my life I took things very positively and never did anything wrong at all.

NOW I HAVE UNDERSTOOD THE TRUTH
THE CRIMINAL IS THAT OLD LADY AND THAT OLD LADY IS AN EMOTIONLESS PERSON.
HER NAME IS C.G.J.H.P.

C: Comparison
G: Greediness
J: Jealousy
H: Hatred
P: Pain

THAT CRIMINAL IS KNOWN AS GODDESS OF

NEGATIVITY AND AN EMOTIONLESS PERSON
WHO TAKE THINGS VERY NEGATIVELY.

ONLY YOU CAN DEFEAT CONNIE BECAUSE YOU
HAVE MADE THAT CRIMINAL EMOTIONAL.
THAT CRIMINAL HAS GOTTEN EMOTIONS
NOW.
THAT'S THE REASON ONLY YOU CAN DEFEAT
HER CONNIE.
ONLY YOU CAN…….

Connie was silent and she was minding her own
business and revealed one single truth to James that the
partner of that old lady was me that is; Connie but she
thought;

THAT OLD LADY WHO ACCEPTED ME.
THAT OLD LADY WHO SUPPORTED ME.
THAT OLD LADY WHO TOOK CARE OF ME ALL
THIS TIME.
AND THAT OLD LADY ONLY IS THE CRIMINAL.
AND I HAVE TO FIGHT WITH THAT PERSON.
WHY…….?

She didn't said a word to SMOSH but casually asked
that what happened to you.
SMOSH replied that back then even I was also not able
to understand anything that what was going wrong with
me but now I have understood everything.

THE TRUTH IS:

I was not comparing, getting greedy or becoming jealous of anyone. I was controlled to feel that way.

In other words, I was being controlled to get this kind of emotions.

My face changed many times, no doubt about it but the truth was that I was internally dying and I was not changing my faces consciously or subconsciously, I was internally dying and then my face was changing and now my face is like a young man.

I was being hypnotized to focus completely to think as if you will get senses and I gotten a supernatural ability that I will get senses.

THE CRIMINAL IS C.G.J.H.P.

NOW I HAVE UNDERSTOOD THE TRUTH HOW I GOTTEN PREGNANT.

I HAVE GOTTEN PREGNANT THROUGH HYPNOTISM.

I was hypnotized and I was made to get senses. I thought so much about as if I am sleeping with someone whole time. Every time every moment, only that thing used to get in my head and then I was hypnotized to see the eye of that criminal.

The look that eye, it was so strong that my eyes became very big, the eye ball became very very larger and my eyes started shivering like a hell. That's the reason whenever I see me myself, that look comes whenever I see my face.

MY SENSES ARE SO STRONG THAT IT TURNED INTO REALITY.

SMOSH removed his cloth and showed his body.
Seeing his body, VOSS gotten shocked. The body was full of rods which were stabbed here and there.
She asked that how you gotten that and how are you alive.
SMOSH said very casually.

I WAS HYPNOTISED TO STAB ME MYSELF WITH THESE RODS.
THIS IS THE TRUTH.

VOSS gotten shocked and gotten very angry with full of eyes turning red and blood was rushing here and there.
She said one single word and that was; I will never forgive that criminal.

Beauty Made For Each other

E VERYONE CAME
  INTRODUCE YOURSELF

SMOSH
GABE
GROSS
HAG
MOST
CAGE
GAN
VOSS

VOSS said to everyone that how you all are linked to C.G.J.H.P and what that person did to you.

1. SMOSH showed his body that his body was full of stabbed rods.

. GABE was forced to marry that criminal without her willingness. GROSS was being used by that criminal and that criminal did a wrong thing using his money and he was criticized a lot.

. HAG was forced to have sex with that criminal without his willingness.
. MOST was being used by that enemy to kill those people who were actually good people but forced to kill them as ordered by that enemy.
. CAGE used to make lots of jokes with that criminal, but that criminal laughed at him bad intentionally and made him a laughing stock in front of the entire world.
. GAN was tortured by that criminal/enemy by making him drown and by making him stopping his breath and that's why he wants to kill him very very badly.
. VOSS was experimented and that's why she gotten a third eye on her forehead.

WE ALL WILL KILL THIS CRIMINAL.
WE ALL WILL……
LET'S GO
SMOSH AND VOSS
GABE AND HAG
MOST AND GAN
GROSS AND CAGE

THE MEETING OVER
HAG was looking GABE very weirdly and gently talked to her. GABE was minding her own business that time, but she said," Can you really understand my feelings?"

HAG in a very flirtatiously way said that Ya I can.
I am the most handsome man and you are the most beautiful girl and only those people can understand them who have faced the same faith.
We both are beautiful and of course we both can understand each other.
Come on let's have a talk now.

GABE nicely said," Generally each and everyone like to be the most beautiful people never seen before, but my problem is that only that I am the most beautiful person. How ironical is this….
I always wanted a true friendship, a true love, a true everything and that only I am not getting."

HAG very laughingly said that the same condition even for me also. There are so many girls who are chasing after me so many times that I am not at all getting a trustworthy person at all.

For us, both the conditions are same only.
Don't you think that you know,
We are in the same condition.
We both are beautiful.
We are able to understand each other.

WHAT IS YOUR SAYING?

GABE thought something and just agreed.

What kind of romantic moment it was.
AMAZING….

Generally , it is said that only and only people can help and understand those people only who have faced the same faith because they only know what and how it feels when you are in that pain .

It is very easy to say but very hard to do.
This is the truth.

When people say that they can do anything to help you but as there is a moral "A friend in need is a friend indeed."

And that usually works when both of them have faced the same faith, the same pain.

Only those people generally are able to understand each other and can help each other.

Strong Nature, Strong Bond

One day, GAN was feeling very nice and free and the leaves were falling, the wind was chill and everything was going very well. MOST comes and starts talking to him.

MOST asked," Why are you always chasing after Nature that much?"

GAN replied that from the very beginning I was in love with nature. I used to see grasses and trees.

I was such a person back then that I was even feared to touch the grass thinking that grass will get hurt.

I am so in love with nature that I used to cry when someone used to hurt them. But GAN tried to save himself saying that I used to think that way back then but not now.

MOST understood him and said that you know everything cannot be perfectly good and if they seems as if they are perfectly good, there must be a darkness hidden inside of them.

Now you only think, no doubt nature puts effort so that

everyone will get everything but even this much also nature is not that bad and not that good.

That's why Tsunami and earthquake occurs.
That's why it's been said that Nature is cruel.
GAN was about to get angry but when he heard that nature is cruel, he became silent and thought of VOSS's words that nature is cruel only and only because they have gotten emotions for you or otherwise they wouldn't have been.

GAN nicely replied that no doubt because of nature, I was harmed also but you know what to do, I am still in love with nature. It feels as if nature is my lover.

But for some reason, GAN minded his own business.

GAN nicely asked, "What are your abilities MOST?"
MOST said, "Well I am a very strong person that I can handle to destroy the whole land".
MOST talked about himself.

Back then , I was a very weak person and completely untalented person also. I didn't knew anything about it and completely clueless about each and everything. But I really worked hard like a hell and because of this strong nature of stubbornness and my hard work, I have became a very strong person.

GAN said only and only one single thing and that is;

you have a strong nature of your stubbornness and I have a strong bond towards my nature which makes me a stubborn person.

It's been said that nature is very strong and the bond for nature that GAN has is also very strong.

A deep love for the nature makes the nature strong and its bond also.

MOST became a very strong person because of his effort and the strong nature he had to become a strong person, ready to do anything to reach his goal.

A strong bond, A strong nature……

Crazy and Richness

GROSS and CAGE were walking like that only.

GROSS tried to tease CAGE saying that you comedians do nothing except making crazy and funny jokes, right. CAGE nicely understood GROSS and said ," You know, we comedians no doubt make lots of crazy jokes but at least we do for our survival and entertaining others , at least we don't boast about money or like that kind of thing".

GROSS gotten very angry but somehow he controlled himself and asked him to tell details about comedians. CAGE replied that no doubt we comedians do nothing except entertaining
people but see the outcomes also that they are getting from us.
They are enjoying.
They are having fun.
They are happy.
Even we are also getting our affordable money for our survival.

But we comedians look very funny, very crazy but even we also have gotten lots and lots of pain nesting inside our heart.
We are being called jokers, cartoons, etc whatever it is and we have to face insult for our survival.
You only say what shall we do now.
You tease we comedians, no doubt about it but what about our feelings.
No one understands that.

GROSS replied," No doubt about it but for some reason I can understand your feelings.
You know what happens to us, we will tell you that now.
We rich people have a certain procedure how to stay and how to do our day to day life activities.
We rich people have a particular way to behave, our manners, our way of talking, our way of eating, etc.
Each and everything is being looked and observed.
We rich people are forced to live like that and not allowed to be casually talking to others the way other common people do.
This is our hell or our heaven, who knows about it.

CAGE said only and only one single thing that I am crazy for entertaining people and became rich for entertaining people and you are rich in showing or expressing others.

All the people are same and equivalent.

Their behaviour or way of reacting can be different, but people are one and this world is united.

CAGE is a comedian, but he is rich for creating jokes and crazy to entertain people while GROSS is a rich person and crazy to express his richness.

Tough Planning

Everyone assembles
VOSS starts speaking

VOSS told her entire story to each and everyone.
A long back years ago, when I was being taken care by that old lady I was hearing lots of voices.
The real truth is that I was the partner of C.G.J.H.P.
Back then , I was very simple and innocent girl but I was being used by that old lady and I became a very very violent person. This is my truth.

EVERYONE BECAME SILENT.

VOSS relied,
"THE ONE WHO TOOK CARE OF ME.
THE ONE WHO GAVE ME EVERYTHING.
THE ONE WHO ACCEPTED ME AND NOW I UNDERSTOOD THAT SHE WAS THE ONE WHO RUINED ME NOW".

EVERYONE SAID ONLY AND ONLY ONE SINGLE WORD AND THAT IS;

C.G.J.H.P.………
WE WILL NOT FORGIVE YOU……
NEVER.

SMOSH minded his own business and said everyone to deal with that criminal now.

Now everyone listen to me, I have a plan how to deal with C.G.J.H.P.

Everyone have to regain their skills. Become very very violent person.
Use your skills very very smartly.
. Forget your sympathy and your past.
. Fight as if it is your likeness or your life.

I have some clues also.
C.G.J.H.P. is a very smart person.
I bet that she will change faces according to the ability or strength we have and making those kind of faces which will prevent us to fight with that particular person.

In 3.2.1……
Step by step I will tell the truth or details as if how she will fight with each and everyone.

FOR MOST,
C.G.J.H.P. can try to form herself into a child so that you won't use your monstrous strength in front of that kid.

FOR GABE,
She will turn herself into a man.

FOR HAG,
A beautiful woman

FOR GROSS,
A beggar

FOR CAGE,
A crying person

FOR GAN,
Person who ruined the nature.

FOR VOSS
C.G.J.H.P. herself.

AND FINALLY FOR ME
FOR SMOSH
A person having lots of guns.

SO IN
3_2_1
ARE YOU ALL READY FOR IT……..

EVERYONE'S ANSWER
WE ALL ARE READY FOR IT.

The Fight Begins___ Come On…..

A FTER 6 YEARS……..

THE TIME HAS CAME NOW……
C.G.J.H.P. ARE YOU READY…..?

THE PARTY IS GOING TO START NOW……

ASSEMBLE

SMOSH
GABE
HAG
GROSS
CAGE
GAN
MOST
VOSS

They have regained their skills and these members have improved also and are ready to fight with C.G.J.H.P.

THE ABILITIES OF THESE MEMBERS ARE:

SMOSH:
Very strong person. Look is very scary.
. Uses his stabbed rods to fight plus his external and internal soldiers.

GABE:
Very beautiful.. Attractive.
. Uses her long hair to fight.

HAG:
Very handsome man.
Very smart person.
Uses his beauty to make others follow him.

GROSS:
Very rich person. . Fearless man
. Made external soldiers to fight.

CAGE:
1.Very scary guy
?. Violent fighter plus very scary laughter
@. Gotten some weapons and fighting continuously without getting exhausted.

GAN:
>. Nature lover
?. Very fearful scream

@. Takes help from nature to fight.

MOST
>. Having muscles ?. Violent look
@. Strong enough to break the land.
VOSS:
>. Violent eyes
?. Stubbornness and good observational skills
@. Violent fighter, uses her third eye plus having external and internal soldiers.

WE ALL HAVE GATHERED TOGETHER TO KILL YOU C.G.J.H.P.
LET THE PARTY BEGIN NOW…..
UNDERSTOOD….
LET'S GO…

VOSS said that I know where we will meet that C.G.J.H.P.

WORDS SAID BY EVERYONE…
"THE HEADQUARTER WHICH LIES IN UNDERGROUND PACIFIC OCEAN."

All these members with their weapons, external and internal soldiers twent underground by a submarine.
When they reached underground water, they saw an imaginary world which was created by that criminal.
The imaginary world was exactly like a real world and they were able to go to that place.

It was exactly like a mirage which can be felt or touched.

They went inside and found out that there were millions of internal and external soldiers and there was a headquarter.
They were exactly like real people only.
Those members were hidden and GROSS, VOSS AND SMOSH took care of external soldiers and SMOSH and VOSS took care of internal soldiers.

They went inside that headquarter and they found out something which was:

"Full of blood and blood
As if their food is blood
Making that place
As a red ocean".

THE TIME HAS CAME.
FOUND YOU FINALLY.....
FOUND YOU.........

THE ENEMY HAS CAME.....

"What a terrible face
Like a drinking blood body
Full of blood
As if cannot live
WITHOUT BLOOD".

VOSS said,"Oh BLOOD. Even this word can be put like this".

B:BETTER
L:LOOK YOURSELF
O:OWE
O: OTHERS
D: AND DON'T TRY TO RUIN THEM

GOOD INTENTIONALLY……………….

FINALLY THAT CRIMINAL CAME {C.G.J.H.P}….

There were many soldiers who were looking very scary and there were some internal and external soldiers also.
Finally the main criminal came that is; C.G.J.H.P with her members who were;
>. A child
?. Man @. Beggar
N. A crying person O. Woman
P. A man who ruined the nature
Q. A person with full of weapons.
VOSS had 7 members having weapons plus some external and internal soldiers also.

FIGHT BEGINS…..

MOST vs CHILD

The CHILD was looking very innocent and childish person.

"What an innocent person
Removing the fear of getting angry
Being caused by everyone".

MOST
"What an anger
That makes the entire place
To shiver
Very fearfully".
MOST showed that child such an angry face that the child was not able to cry also and the child gotten defeated immediately.

____

GABE vs MAN

The MAN was reacting as if he needs a woman who can do each and everything for him.

"Please help me
Need for a woman
Who will take care of this
Man forever".

GABE
"What an attractive look

The beauty of her hair
Make demons
To kill themselves".

GABE nicely came close saying that a need for woman ,
right so I came and she gently took her hair and pressed
his neck by using her long hair to make that man never
even thinking of asking about a woman.

GROSS vs BEGGAR

BEGGAR was very poor person and had no money to
survive. So he was asking for a support.

"What a pitiful face
I have
No money for survival
Please help me".

GROSS
"What a man
Having no fear
Made his external soldiers
To fight for him fearlessly".

GROSS nicely said in such a way that the beggar was
not able to ask for help to him at all saying that you
beggars instead of making good quotes or dialogue,

why don't you start working and use your energy in that instead of talking and making dialogues.

___

CAGE vs CRYING PERSON

That CRYING PERSON was such a person who had no reaction of smiling and somehow he wanted someone who can entertain that person.

"No happiness
Please help me
No sympathy
What to do
Tell me…".

CAGE

"What a scary laugh
What a fighter
Make demons
To die laughingly".

CAGE nicely said ," Oh , you want sympathy do one thing make your food sympathy, understood and don't try to put a chance atlas in front of me. Got it".

___

HAG vs WOMAN

The WOMAN was such a person who just by seeing him was not able to bear to flirt him.

"Flirtation never stops
How much I try
What to do when
I already seen your face".

HAG
"How handsome
What a smartness
Make demons to angels

To fight for him".
HAG showed such an expression that without those angels only, that woman immediately died.

GAN vs PERSON WHO RUINED THE NATURE

The PERSON WHO RUINED THE NATURE was so egoistic that he can even overcome nature's anger also.

"Nature cannot ruin me
We are the ones
Who gave them everything
What will you do now".

GAN

"What a godly figured person
For nature
Makes the nature
To help him immediately".

GAN said," If we are the supporters, then nature is a protector and we all are equivalent . So don't try to even think about ruining it".

SMOSH vs A PERSON FULL OF WEAPONS

That PERSON WHO IS FULL OF WEAPONS was reacting in such a way that as if he is only a weapon.

"My body is weapon
me myself is a weapon
Ready to fight
Weapon vs weapon".

SMOSH
"What a scary body
Using those stabbed rods
To kill each and everyone
For revenge".

FINALLY THE FIGHT BEGINS
VOSS vs C.G.J.H.P

STARTING OF THE FIGHT

C.G.J.H.P
"Cruel eyes
Shouting as the blood rushes
making the hands to reach the ground
Fighting like an animal".

VOSS
"Eyes shivering
Blood rushing
Through her eyes
Ready for this fight".

FIGHT BEGINS

C.G.J.H.P
"Running like an animal
Biting here and there
Hair fully ruined
Stabbing with her teeth".

VOSS
"Eyes made to see
Here and there
Stabbing with rod
Using hair to press the neck
Using nails to make the blood rush
Biting and pulling that demon's hair

Making the fight cruel and violent".

EVERY ONE COMES
CHASING AFTER THAT CRIMINAL
TAKING HER AT ONE SIDE
AND MAKING HER TO STOP MOVING.
MOST
MAKING HER TO STOP MOVING.

GABE
USING HER HAIR TO PRESS THE NECK.

GROSS
PICKING HER HAND.

HAG
LOOKING IN FRONT OF HER TO EXPRESS HIS
BEAUTY.

GAN
TAKING HELP FROM NATURE TO MAKE HER
STOP BREATHING.

CAGE
SHOWING HIS CRUEL SMILE.

SMOSH
STABBING HER LEG THROUGH A ROD.

EVERYONE SAYS:

COME VOSS…..
COME………

FINALLY THE TIME HAS CAME
VOSS COMES.

"The one
Who did everything
Who accepted my truth
Who was my first light
Is going to sleep permanently
In front of me".

VOSS take a rod and comes.

IN 3_2_1_
HAAAAAAAAA

VOSS stabs C.G.J.H.P
IT'S OVER..

C.G.J.H.P DIES BUT BEFORE DYING SHE SHOWS
ONE SMILING EXPRESSION TO VOSS AND DIES
PERMANENTLY
OLD LADY, DON'T WORRY.
PEOPLE DON'T DIE
THEIR EXPERIENCES, THEIR MOMENTS ALWAYS
LIES INSIDE OUR HEART.
YOU WILL NEVER DIE FOR ME OLD LADY. NEVER.

VOSS licks her blood and goes away and the entire securities came.

MOST
GABE
GROSS
CAGE
HAG
GAN
SMOSH
VOSS

YOU HAVE SAVED OUR WORLD.
YOU ALL WILL BE KNOWN AS GODS AND GODDESSES OF OUR WORLD.

The entire people clapped for them.

The Upcoming of Our Gods And Goddesses

THE SECURITIES ARE THERE
THERE IS A HUGE CROWD WAITING FOR THEM.

NOW OUR GODS AND OUR GODDESSES HAVE CAME.

IN 3_2_1…

ASSEMBLE

MOST
GABE
GROSS
CAGE
HAG
GAN
SMOSH
VOSS

All the securities brought them as if they are kings or queens and took a very good care for them.
All the dressing clothes everything was ready.
For women , there was a dress like kimono and the dress was looking very traditional and very very godly.

THESE PEOPLE ARE OUR GODS AND GODDESSES OF OUR ENTIRE WORLD. IN 3_2_1...

THE NAMES ARE:
MOST_THE FIGHTER
GABE_THE BEAUTY QUEEN
GROSS_THE MOST RICHEST MAN
CAGE_THE MOST CRAZIEST PERSON
HAG_THE MOST HANDSOME MAN
GAN_THE NATURE LOVER
SMOSH_THE DANGEROUS MAN
VOSS_THE THIRD EYED WOMAN

HAAAAAAAAAAAAAAAAAAAAAAAAAAA.

Finally all these people were appreciated and became gods and goddesses of the entire world and all these people were accepted by the entire world.

Hoooooooooooooooooooooo.

Conclusion

"This world is one
People staying in this world
Are also one.
This world wants to give
The happiness to all of them
Who stay in this world."

However people are , all the world citizens are one since this entire world is one.

If you have faced that much bad things, that much you will face good things also.

We face lots of challenges but whatever happens, it happens for good only. The only thing to do is to realise.

When we face challenges, we learn a lesson and there is a meaning hidden inside of it.

At last , whatever they were, however they were , they

were accepted and they were acknowledged by each and everyone.

They got acceptance and acknowledgement and they lived life very happily and they became successful in their life.

THE END